NEW AMERICANS

Korean Americans

by William David Thomas

Series Consultant: Judith A. Warner, Ph.D.,
Professor of Sociology and Criminal Justice,
Texas A&M International University

Cavendish Square

Cavendish Square Publishing, LLC
2544 Clinton Street
Buffalo, NY 14224
www.cavendishsq.com

Library of Congress Cataloging-in-Publication Data

Thomas, William David.
Korean Americans / by William David Thomas.
p. cm. — (New Americans)
Includes bibliographical references and index.
ISBN 978-0-7614-4306-3
1. Korean Americans—History—Juvenile literature. 2. Korean Americans--Social conditions—Juvenile literature. 3. Immigrants—United States—History—Juvenile literature. 4. Immigrants—United States—Social conditions—Juvenile literature. 5. United States—Emigration and immigration—Juvenile literature. 6. Korea—Emigration and immigration—Juvenile literature. I. Title.
E184.K6T46 2010
973'.04957--dc22 2008054846

Developed for Cavendish Square Publishing by RJF Publishing LLC
Robert Famighetti, President
www.RJFpublishing.com
Design: Westgraphix LLC/Tammy West
Photo Research: Edward A. Thomas
Map Illustrator: Stefan Chabluk
Index: Nila Glikin

Photo credits: Cover: © Digital Vision/Alamy; 1, 41, 50, 60, 70: Courtesy of Hong Sung Joo; 5, 11, 34, 52: AP/Wide World Photos; 6, 39: © Edward A. Thomas; 12: Courtesy of Daisy Kim; 14:Getty Images; 16: Library of Congress, LC-USZ62-108293; 19: © LEE JAE-WON/Reuters/ Corbis; 20: Library of Congress, LC-DIG-ppmsca-08164; 23: USC Korean American Digital Archive; 27, 32: © Bettmann/CORBIS; 28: Signal Corps Photo #FEC-50-9336; 30: © David Butow/Corbis; 44: © Lee Snider/Photo Images/CORBIS; 46: UNG YEON-JE/AFP/Getty Images; 54: © Nik Wheeler/CORBIS; 57: www.jhoonrhee.com; 59: With the permission of Clarion Books; 61: © Nir Elias/Reuters/Corbis; 62: © Duomo/CORBIS; 66: © Matt Rainey/Star Ledger/ Corbis.

Cover: Several generations of a Korean-American family.

Printed in the United States of America

135642

CONTENTS

Words defined in the glossary are in **bold** type the first time they appear in the text.

INTRODUCTION

The United States has embraced immigration for most of its history—and has been a destination of choice for people seeking a better life. Today hundreds of thousands of immigrants arrive each year to live and work and make their way in a new country. These "New Americans" come for many reasons, and they come from places all over the world. They bring with them new customs, languages, and traditions—and face many challenges in their adopted country. Over time, they and their children are changed by and become part of the American mainstream culture. At the same time, the mainstream is itself changed as it absorbs many elements of the immigrants' cultures, from ethnic foods to ideas from non-Western belief systems. An understanding of the New Americans, and how they will form part of the American future, is essential for everyone.

This series focuses on recent immigrants from eight major countries and regions: the Caribbean and Central America, China, India and other South Asian countries, Korea, Mexico, Russia and Eastern Europe, Southeast Asia, and West Africa.

Each of these geographic areas is a major source of the millions of immigrants who have come to the United States in the last decades of the twentieth century and the beginning of the twenty-first. For many of these people, the opportunity to move to the United States was opened up by the major

New Americans being sworn in as U.S. citizens.

changes in U.S. immigration law that occurred in the 1960s. For others, the opportunity or imperative to immigrate was triggered by events in their own countries, such as the collapse of Communism in Eastern Europe or civil wars in Central America.

Some of the New Americans found sizable communities of Americans from the same ethnic background and had the benefit of "ethnic neighborhoods" to move into where they could feel welcome and get help adjusting to American life. Many of these communities originated in a previous major wave of immigration, from the 1880s to 1920. Some of the New Americans found very few predecessors to ease the transition as they faced the challenges of adjustment.

These volumes tell the stories of the New Americans, including the personal accounts of a number of immigrants and their children who agreed to be interviewed by some of the authors. As you read, you will learn about the countries of origin and the cultures of these newcomers to American society. You will learn, as well, about how the New Americans are enriching, as they adapt to, American life.

Judith A. Warner, Ph.D.
Professor of Sociology and Criminal Justice
Texas A&M International University

Signs are in Korean and restaurants have a Korean flavor in this Korean-American neighborhood in New York City.

CHAPTER ONE

The Korean-American Community Today

Meung-Song Paik was only a child when she left Korea with her family in 1904 and sailed to Hawaii. They were traveling thousands of miles to an unfamiliar place where there were few Koreans and almost everyone spoke a language they could not understand. They were going to work on a **plantation**. They became field laborers, and the whole family—including the children—worked long hours, six days a week, in the red-brown soil of Hawaii.

Ninety years later, in April 1994, a Korean man stood on a mound of red-brown soil. Thirty thousand people were watching, but he didn't notice them. He said later that he felt as if the weight of all Korea was resting on his shoulders. He knew that millions of people in his home country wanted him to succeed. And all he had to do was throw a baseball. His name was Chan Ho Park, and he was wearing the uniform of the Los Angeles Dodgers. That night he became the first Korean ever to play in a Major League Baseball game. Fourteen years later, he was still pitching. In 2008, after playing for other teams, Park came back to Los Angeles to again pitch for the Dodgers.

Bookends

The lives of Meung-Song Paik and Chan Ho Park are like bookends. One is at the beginning of the story of Korean **immigration**. The other is in the present day.

Paik and her family were among the first Koreans to enter U.S. territory. They spoke no English, had few skills, and worked in near-slavery for pennies a day. They had few other Koreans with whom they could share their experiences, their sorrows, or their dreams.

Chan Ho Park was a skilled professional athlete. He earned a lot of money, and an **interpreter** helped him with the language. In Los Angeles, Park was part of the largest Korean-American community in the United States. He could shop in stores where Korean was spoken, eat in Korean restaurants, and read Korean-language newspapers. Between these "bookends" are many other stories. Most of them are about hard work, sacrifice, and adapting to change. They are the stories of Korean Americans.

Coming in Waves

Koreans came to the United States in three main "waves." The first was between 1903 and 1905, when workers like

States with the Most Korean Americans

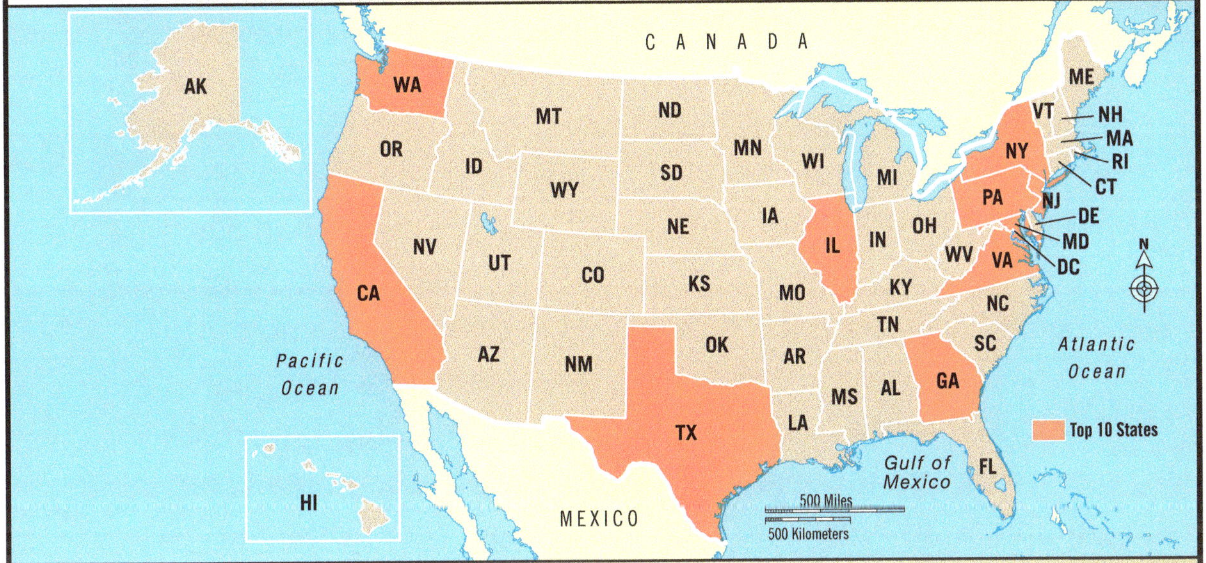

California	345,882
New York	119,846
New Jersey	65,345
Illinois	51,453
Washington	46,880
Texas	45,571
Virginia	45,279
Maryland	39,155
Pennsylvania	31,612
Georgia	28,745

Source: U.S. Bureau of the Census, 2000 Census data.
Note: Census Bureau 2006 population estimates do not give breadowns by state for states with fewer than 65,000 Korean Americans.

Meung-Song Paik's family came to Hawaii. The second wave of immigrants arrived between 1948 and 1964. Wars, changes in government, and a struggling **economy** made them want to leave their homeland. The third wave was by far the largest. It began in 1965 when U.S. immigration law changed. In the next thirty-five years, almost 800,000 Koreans came to the United States.

Early **immigrants** settled on the West Coast. Most of them arrived by ship. Port cities like Los Angeles and San Francisco, in California, and Seattle, in Washington, were natural "gateways" to America. The immigrants who came in later years were attracted to these cities because they had established Korean-American communities. But jet aircraft allowed them to travel farther and faster. Korean communities also began to grow in Chicago, New York, and other cities in the Midwest and on the East Coast.

By the Numbers

The U.S. **Census** Bureau estimated that in 2006 more than 1,335,000 Korean Americans were living in the United States. Three-quarters of them were born in Korea, and for 80 percent of them, Korean was the main language spoken at home. The average age of Korean Americans is a bit younger than the average for the U.S. population as a whole. More than 90 percent of Korean American adults have a high-school diploma—that's higher than the figure for all Americans. Overall, Korean Americans have slightly higher family incomes than most Americans. But not all Korean Americans are well off. Those who don't have a

Chan Ho Park, the first Korean in Major League Baseball, pitches for the Los Angeles Dodgers in September 2008.

Korean immigrant Kim Hyung-Soon created the nectarine. The fruit is now sold across the United States and around the world.

good job or the education and skills to get one are often poor. In fact, the percentage of Korean Americans living in poverty (as defined by the U.S. government) is also slightly higher than for Americans as a whole.

Almost one-third of all Korean Americans were living in California—more than 430,000 people in 2006—and the part of Los Angeles known as Koreatown is the largest

Korean-American neighborhood in the United States. About one in ten Korean Americans was living in New York, many of them in the New York City area, and more than 6 percent were living in New Jersey. Other states with sizable numbers of Korean Americans included Illinois, Washington, Texas, and Virginia.

People

The numbers provide some important information about Korean Americans. But to fully understand the Korean-American community requires more than numbers. You need to know about people's lives.

Kim Hyung-Soon immigrated to Hawaii in the early 1900s. Later he moved on to California, where he worked in the fruit orchards. After starting his own farm, Kim began experimenting with different kinds of peaches. He crossed a peach with a plum and created the first nectarine. Today, Americans spend more than $85 million buying nectarines grown in the United States.

Sammy Lee was born to Korean parents in California in 1920. He became a champion diver in college and went on to medical school.

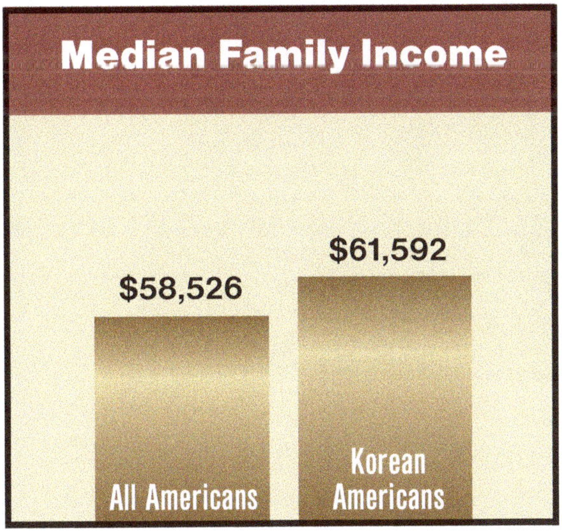

Source: U.S. Bureau of the Census, 2006 estimates

Football star Hines Ward with his mother, Kim Young-Hee, during a visit to South Korea in 2006, shortly after Ward was named Super Bowl MVP.

In 1948, he won gold and bronze medals in the Olympic Games. He won another gold medal in the 1952 Olympics. Lee also served as a major in the U.S. Army Medical Corps. After leaving the Army, Lee continued his medical practice and coached young divers.

Shinae Chun was born and went to college in Korea. She came to the United States to continue her education. Eventually, Chun became Special Assistant to the Governor of Illinois on Asian American Affairs. In 2001, the U.S. Senate confirmed her as Director of the Women's Bureau, part of the Department of Labor. Chun became the highest-ranking Korean American in the U.S. government.

Hines Ward was born in South Korea in 1976, the son of an African-American soldier and a Korean mother. He came to the United States with his family at the age of one. Ward became a star football player with the Pittsburgh Steelers. He was named Most Valuable Player (MVP) in the Super Bowl in 2006. In 2009, he caught two passes in the Steelers' Super Bowl victory.

Paull Shin was an orphan, living on the streets of Korea, begging for food. At the end of the Korean War (1950–1953), he was adopted by an American soldier named Ray Paull and came to the United States. Shin knew little English, but he soon earned a high school diploma. He went on to college and earned a doctorate from the University of Washington. In 1992, he was elected to the Washington House of Representatives. In 1998, he was elected to the State Senate.

These are Korean Americans. In farming, football, and other fields, they are contributing to American life today.

The first Korean Americans worked on sugarcane plantations in Hawaii. Here, workers load cut sugarcane into carts.

CHAPTER TWO

EARLIER GENERATIONS

Koreans refer to their country as Choson. That means "the land of the morning calm." Korea's history, however, has been anything but calm. For thousands of years, Korea was a group of small, warring kingdoms. These kingdoms were finally united in 668 C.E. Korea was then ruled by a series of **dynasties**. These were families from which the king was chosen, generation after generation. The Koryo Dynasty (935–1392) was the source of the name *Korea*.

Japanese Aggression

Korea's early history, customs, and **culture** were heavily influenced by its much larger neighbor, China. Korea is a **peninsula** in east Asia, and China shares a long land border with Korea. Russia, however, is also just to the north, and just to the east (across the narrow Sea of Japan, or East Sea) is the island nation of Japan. Until the mid-1800s, Korea resisted trade and contact with all other countries except China. Western countries began calling Korea "the **Hermit** Kingdom."

During the 1800s, though, Japan was becoming stronger and much more **militant**. In 1876, Japan forced Korea to begin trading. The Japanese government continued to make other demands as well. The Korean government was too weak to resist.

Some Koreans—especially students and other young people—**protested** the government policies that favored Japan. Many people were arrested, and others left Korea in order to avoid prison.

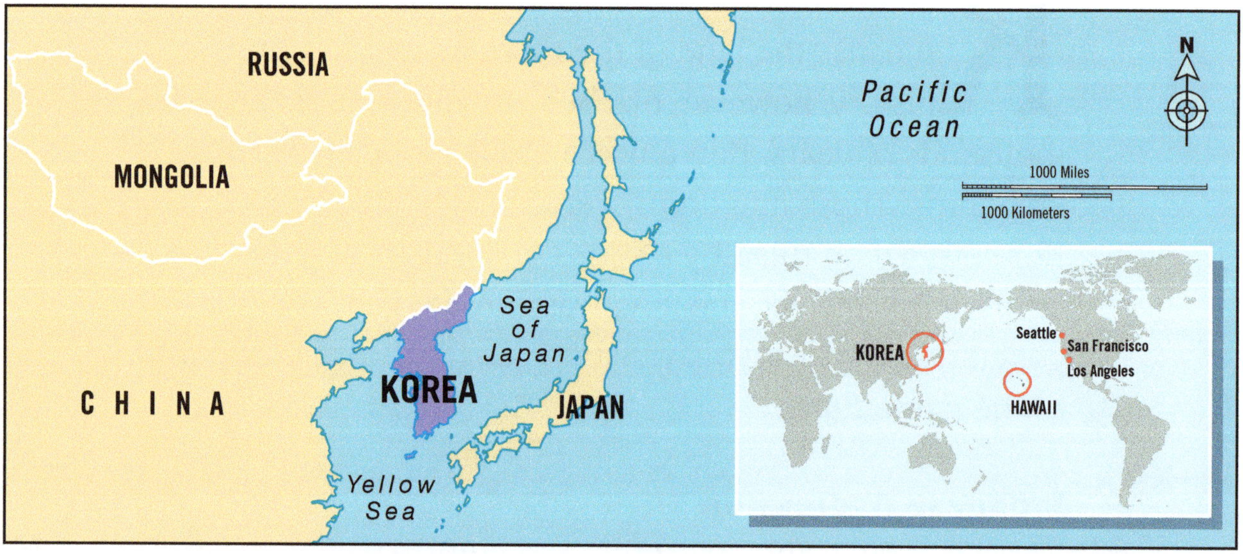

Korea's history and culture have been affected by its more powerful neighbors—China, Russia, and Japan. Koreans who immigrated to Hawaii or to cities on the West Coast of the U.S. mainland traveled thousands of miles from home.

In 1882, Korea agreed to trade with the United States. Soon afterward, Christian **missionaries** from the United States arrived in Korea. In addition to churches, they began setting up schools. The first Korean immigrants to the United States were three college students—political **refugees**—who arrived in 1885.

Japanese armies invaded Korea in 1895. The Japanese seized crops, took over other parts of the Korean economy, forced Koreans to work for them, and even made them adopt Japanese names. Korea eventually turned to Russia for help. (China had just been defeated in a war with Japan and was too weak to help.) Russia and Japan fought a war, in part for control of the Korean peninsula, in 1904–1905. When Japan won the Russo-Japanese War, it gained complete control of Korea. In 1910, Korea was officially made a colony of Japan. The people of Korea suffered greatly from war and foreign control. Some wanted

The Rose of Sharon

In the same way as people associate the shamrock with Ireland, many Koreans link the rose of Sharon with Korea. Its Korean name is *mugunghwa*. The root of the word means "immortal" or "eternal." The ancient Chinese called Korea "the land of gentlemen where mugunghwa blooms." In the early 1900s, when Korean workers were being recruited, they were told that America was "a garden of mugunghwa." Today, the rose of Sharon is the national flower of Korea. It grows in many gardens, and it appears in artwork, clothing, postcards, and postage stamps.

This woman is holding a rose of Sharon, Korea's national flower.

Japanese soldiers warm themselves by a fire after a 1904 battle in the Russo-Japanese War.

to leave to escape danger and hardships. At the same time, sugarcane growers in the Hawaiian islands were looking for workers.

To Hawaii

Hawaii became a territory of the United States in 1898. Americans owned many of the large sugarcane plantations on these islands, which are in the mid–Pacific Ocean, about 2,500 miles (4,000 kilometers) southwest of California and some 4,500 mi. (7,200 km) southeast of Korea. In the early 1900s the sugarcane growers began recruiting Koreans to work on their plantations. They described Hawaii as a paradise, and the United States as a land where dreams come true. Workers were told they would receive good pay, free housing, health care, and English lessons. American missionaries told Koreans that living in the United States would make them better Christians.

The first Korean workers arrived in Hawaii in 1903. Nearly seven thousand came during the next two years. They found that things were not as they had been promised. Instead of good housing and medical care, they found leaky shacks, hard work, and few doctors.

A typical work day could start as early as 5 AM and last for ten hours or more. A day's pay was less than seventy cents. The work was back breaking, and supervisors kept close watch to make sure Korean laborers did not take breaks. Often, supervisors did not know—or care to learn—the workers' names. Each worker carried a number and was called by number.

Picture Brides

By 1905, Korea was completely controlled by Japan, and **emigration** stopped. The Japanese government would not allow people to leave the peninsula. In 1907, however, the Japanese and American governments signed a paper known as the Gentlemen's Agreement. It said although in general Koreans could not emigrate, wives could join husbands who were already in the United States.

Nearly all of the Koreans in the United States at that time were men, and nearly all of them were unmarried. The Gentlemen's Agreement started a system called "picture brides." Through their families or village **matchmakers**, Korean men in Hawaii exchanged pictures of themselves with women in Korea. When a match was made, the woman sailed to Hawaii to meet her new husband. Sometimes marriage ceremonies were carried out on the ship, so that when the couple stepped onto American soil they were legally married. Between 1910 and 1924, more than a thousand Korean picture brides came to the United States. Most went to Hawaii, though some went to California and elsewhere in the United States. Things didn't always work out well. Many brides found that their husbands were much older than they looked in the pictures they had sent. And the new wives were expected to work in the fields as well.

The "Yellow Peril"

In the mid–1800s, thousands of Chinese workers had immigrated to the United States. Many of them settled in California. They often worked for lower wages than white

Do Yen Kim was a picture bride.
She married Yung Ho Yoon in
San Francisco in 1915.

Americans would accept, and this caused a great deal of **resentment**. Some Americans felt that the Chinese were taking jobs away from them and did not like the growth of Chinese-owned businesses. In 1882, Congress passed the Chinese Exclusion Act. It stopped nearly all immigration from China.

Some Koreans arrived on the West Coast in the early 1900s, and they quickly felt the same resentment and **discrimination** as the Chinese. Restaurants often refused to serve them. In California, gangs of white men **harassed** Korean Americans, and police officers often looked the other way.

Author Jack London, famous for such novels as *White Fang* and *The Call of the Wild*, created a term that summed up the fears of many Americans. In 1904, he wrote a story for a San Francisco newspaper. In it, he claimed that Koreans were lazy and worthless. London's story was titled "The Yellow Peril." Fear of the "yellow peril" led to new, discriminatory laws. California passed a law in 1913 that said Asians could not own land in the state. Other states soon passed similar laws. A law passed by Congress in 1917 prohibited almost all immigration to the United States from Asia.

In the next decade, the U.S. Congress passed a major immigration law. This Immigration Act of 1924 (also called the Johnson-Reid Act or the National Origins Act) set **quotas**, or limits, by country on the number of immigrants allowed to enter the United States. A country's quota was 2 percent of the number of people from that country already living in the United States in 1890. Because so few Koreans had come to the United States before 1890, the new law allowed almost no immigration from Korea.

"I Am Korean"

For the United States, World War II began on December 7, 1941. On that morning, Japanese aircraft bombed the U.S. Navy base at Pearl Harbor, in Hawaii. Koreans still felt anger toward the Japanese for invading their homeland. But since Korea was a colony of Japan, Koreans living in the United States were classified as Japanese citizens. That meant they were officially "enemy aliens" once the United States was at war with Japan. Korean Americans were also the victims of some of the strong anti-Japanese feelings many Americans had during the war. To remind people that they were not Japanese, many Korean Americans began wearing arm patches with the Korean flag or the words "I am Korean" on them.

World War II and the Korean War

During World War II (1939–1945), the Japanese still ruled Korea. They forced Koreans to work in factories and mines to help the war effort. When the United States entered the war in 1941, Koreans welcomed this event. They believed that a U.S. victory would drive the Japanese out of Korea. Japan surrendered in 1945, and Koreans celebrated in the streets. But at least for some, the freedom they dreamed of did not appear.

Russia (then called the Union of Soviet Socialist Republics, or Soviet Union)—an ally of the United States in World War II—sent troops and tanks into Korea just as the war was ending. Soon after, the former allies became opponents in what is known as the cold war—a global rivalry for power and influence between the United States and the Soviet Union that lasted for more than forty years. In the early days of the cold war, the United States and the Soviet Union essentially divided Korea. In 1948, two countries were officially established. North Korea (the Democratic People's Republic of Korea) had a **Communist** government, supported by the Soviet Union and China, that was an **oppressive** dictatorship. South Korea (the Republic of Korea), which was backed by the United States, formed a more democratic government—though at times it limited opposition to the government and cracked down on protestors.

Korea was divided after World War II. The North became a Communist country. South Korea had a more democratic government.

In 1950, North Korea invaded South Korea. The United States and other nations sent troops to defend the South. China sent troops to fight with the North Koreans. The Korean War lasted for three years. As many as 4 million people were killed or wounded. But in the end, neither side won. In the truce ending the war in 1953, Korea remained divided, North and South, essentially as it had been before the fighting started.

Syngman Rhee (1875–1965)

Syngman Rhee was one of Korea's great patriots. He is sometimes called "the father of modern Korea." Rhee went to an American missionary high school in Korea. He became a believer in democracy. He joined a group that wanted Korea to be free from Japanese influence. Because Japan already had so much control over Korea by this time, Rhee was arrested, tortured, and imprisoned. He became a Christian while in prison. When he was released, in 1904, he fled to the United States. With help from missionaries, Rhee studied at top American universities. He returned to Korea in 1911 but had to flee from the Japanese once more. Rhee moved to Hawaii, where he taught, gave speeches, and published articles. He became a leader of the Korean community there. After World War II, Rhee returned to Korea and tried to stop the division of his country. His efforts failed, but Rhee was elected the first president of South Korea. He served four terms as president (1948–1960), and he continued, though unsuccessfully, to push for the reunification of Korea.

Syngman Rhee, shown here in 1953, was the first president of South Korea. He wanted his country to remain united.

U.S. soldiers in combat during the Korean War (1950–1953). About 140,000 Americans were killed or wounded in the war.

The Littlest Immigrants

The Korean War left thousands of children without parents. And in the following years, hard economic times forced some Korean parents to abandon newborn children. The South Korean government allowed foreigners to adopt these orphaned children. At one point, one percent of all South Korean newborns were being adopted and leaving the country. The South Korean government began to phase out the practice in 1987, but it started up again in 1998. Between 1953 and 1987, more than 60,000 Korean children were adopted by American families. By 2006, the total number of Korean children adopted and brought to the United States was around 100,000.

The McCarran-Walter Act

In general, immigration from South Korea increased slightly during the 1950s; the North Korean government would not allow emigration. The increase came after the U.S. Congress passed the Immigration and Nationality Act of 1952 (also called the McCarran-Walter Act). The new law kept the national immigration quotas, but it also gave some **preference** to immigrants who were well educated or had needed skills. As a result, some Korean nurses came to work in the United States, along with a few **engineers** and doctors. Also, the United States kept thousands of troops in South Korea after the Korean War. Some American soldiers stationed there married local women, and when the soldiers returned home, these women were permitted to enter the United States as "war brides."

By the 1960s, though, the Korean-American population was still quite small. According to U.S. government figures, fewer than 23,000 Koreans came to the United States between 1903 and 1964. But a surge in immigration was coming.

Korean-American teens shop for CDs at a music store in Koreatown, in Los Angeles.

CHAPTER THREE

THE NEW IMMIGRANTS

When the Korean War ended, the whole peninsula was in **shambles**. Factories, roads, bridges, and farms had been destroyed. An estimated one million **civilians** had been killed. The young nation of South Korea, with help from the United States and other countries, began to rebuild.

The 1960s and 1970s were times of great change in South Korea. Its economy moved from one based mostly on farming to one based on **manufacturing**. Modern factories began turning out clothing, tools, and electronic goods. An automotive industry started up, too, producing cars, small trucks, and tires. Most of these goods were made to be sold in other countries.

Seoul, the capital of South Korea, suffered terrible damage during the Korean War.

The factory workers were not paid well. Low wages for workers meant that Korean products could be sold more cheaply. That made them attractive to buyers overseas. The government also discouraged **unions** and made strikes by workers illegal. This, too, kept workers' pay low.

The South Korean government also regulated the price of rice—the basic food of the nation. The price was kept low to help families, but soon rice growers could not earn enough money to keep their farms. They began moving to cities, looking for factory jobs. But as more people left their farms, factory jobs became harder to find.

South Korea's population was growing rapidly as well. By the mid–1960s there were not enough jobs to go around. This was true not just for factory jobs. Even highly trained professionals—doctors, engineers, and scientists—faced a shortage of good jobs in South Korea. They began looking for work in other countries. And the country they looked to most was the United States.

"Contributions We Need"

The 1960s were times of change in the United States as well. The Vietnam War was beginning, and African Americans were demanding equal rights. Immigration laws were changing, too. In 1964, U.S. Attorney General Robert Kennedy wrote a letter to the *New York Times*. "The time

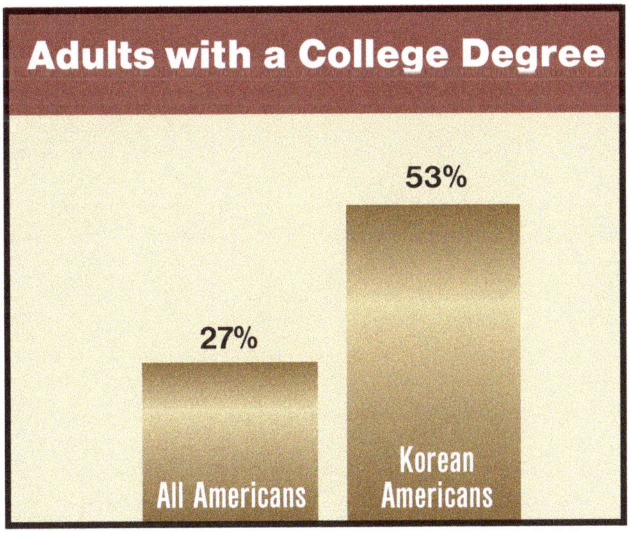

Source: U.S. Bureau of the Census, 2006 estimates

Civil Rights and Immigration

The 1960s were **turbulent** times in the United States. Across the country, African Americans were organizing, marching, and **boycotting** to demand their **civil rights**. For many years they had in effect been denied equal voting rights, the right to live where they wished, and equal treatment in courts. In 1963, hundreds of thousands of people gathered in Washington, D.C., to hear Martin Luther King Jr. deliver his famous "I have a dream" speech. Laws and practices that discriminated against people because of their race were being struck down. Among them were laws that set immigration quotas according to race. The changes made to U.S. immigration law in 1965, ending country-specific quotas, were seen by many people as part of the struggle for civil rights in the United States.

Dr. Martin Luther King Jr., a leader in the struggle for equal rights, gave his famous "I have a dream" speech in Washington, D.C., in 1963.

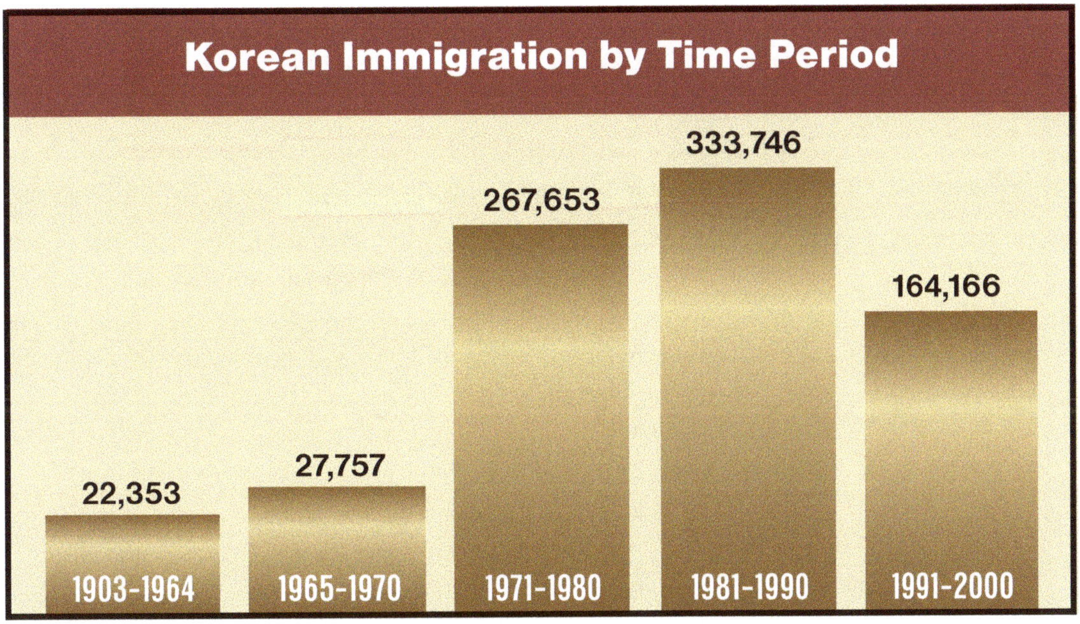

Source: U.S. Immigration and Naturalization Service, 2000

has come for us to insist that the quota system be replaced," he wrote. "It deprives us of able immigrants whose contributions we need."

Supporters of immigration reform got their way when Congress passed the Immigration and Nationality Act of 1965 (also called the Hart-Celler Act). It eliminated the separate quotas for each country. Instead, a total number was set for immigrants from the entire Eastern Hemisphere (the half of the earth that includes Europe, Asia, Africa, and Australia). Within that total number, the new act gave preference to people who were "gifted professionals, scientists, and artists."

Another part of the law became known as the "Brothers and Sisters Act." It said that immediate relatives of U.S.

Timeline: Key Dates in Korean-American Immigration

1885	A few political refugees from Korea arrive in the United States.
1903	The first Korean workers arrive in Hawaii to work on sugarcane plantations; over the next two years, about 7,000 more arrive.
1905	Japan effectively takes control of Korea; all emigration is banned.
1907	A Gentlemen's Agreement between the United States and Japan allows Korean wives of Korean-American immigrants to emigrate; this begins the flow of "picture brides" to Hawaii and elsewhere in the United States.
1913	California passes a law prohibiting Asians from owning land. Several other states soon enact similar laws.
1924	The U.S. Immigration Act of 1924 sets quotas by country for immigrants coming to the United States. Under the law's formula, Korea's quota is extremely low.
1945	At the end of World War II, Japan's control of Korea ends. Russian troops occupy the northern half of Korea; U.S. troops occupy the southern half. Korea is, in effect, divided.
1948	Korea is formally divided into two countries: North Korea and South Korea.
1950–1953	The Korean War: North Korea (later joined by China) attacks South Korea (backed by the United States); the war ends with Korea still divided essentially as it was before the fighting.
1950–1965	Thousands of Korean "war brides" come to the United States; many adopted orphans arrive as well.
1965	Congress passes the Immigration and Nationality Act of 1965, ending country quotas for immigrants to the United States.
1965–1970	More than 27,000 Koreans immigrate to the United States.
1971–1990	More than 600,000 Koreans immigrate to the United States; large Korean-American communities develop in Seattle, San Francisco, New York City, Chicago, and especially Los Angeles.
1991–2000	Although immigration slows, more than 164,000 Koreans come to the United States.
2000–2009	Immigration continues, but at a very slow rate. South Korea's economy gives its citizens opportunities at home.

permanent residents and citizens could come to the United States to join them. Importantly, relatives of U.S. citizens were allowed to immigrate without being counted against the overall immigration quota.

Confucianism

Confucius was a **philosopher** who lived in China about 2,500 years ago. His teachings reached Korea and became the major belief system of the country. Confucianism is not a religion. It is a set of principles that describe good behavior and the ways people should relate to each other. In most cases, Confucianism places the good of society—the family, the community, the country—above the good of the individual. It teaches that a person must have great respect for the elderly, that parents must love their children, and that children must obey their parents. It also teaches honesty and loyalty to the government.

The New Law's Impact

The 1965 act had a dramatic impact on immigration from Korea, paving the way for tens of thousands of South Koreans—particularly those from middle-class and upper-class families—to come to the United States. Their numbers included doctors, nurses, scientists, and skilled technical workers.

Here is a **hypothetical** example of how the new immigration law could work: A Korean chemist applied to come to the United States. Because he was a skilled scientist, his application was given preference. He became one of the applicants from the Eastern Hemisphere who was allowed to immigrate. After settling into life in the United States, the chemist sent for his family. His wife, their two children, and his parents soon joined him. Later, these people could send for other family members to join them. Once immigrants became U.S. citizens, family members they sent for did not count against the total number of immigrants allowed to enter the United States each year.

Although fewer than 23,000 Koreans had come to the United States before 1965, between 1965 and 1990 the number of Korean immigrants was almost 630,000. Immigration then started to slow, at least in part because the economy in South Korea had improved. Even so, 164,000 Koreans came to the United States in the 1990s. Virtually all of the new immigrants came from South Korea, since North Korea's Communist government still would not allow people to leave.

As South Korea's economic strength continued, Korean immigration did decline dramatically in the first decade of the twenty-first century. From 2001 to 2006 the number of Korean immigrants entering the United States was only slightly over 10,000.

Language Barriers, Culture Shock

Like earlier waves of immigrants, the new Korean Americans faced discrimination and difficult adjustments. Many Korean-American children entered schools where the teachers and fellow students spoke a language that, at first, they couldn't understand.

The language barrier was a major issue as well for adults seeking work—and this could be especially true for medical professionals. Immigrant doctors must pass exams before they can practice medicine in the United States. That includes an English language test. Many of the skilled doctors and nurses from Korea could work only as hospital orderlies or aides because their English skills were limited. Those doctors who did pass their exams often found work only in inner-city hospitals (considered by other doctors to be less desirable places to work). Many of the patients there spoke only Spanish. The same problem occurred for engineers and scientists. Despite having needed skills and abilities, some were at least initially unable to find good jobs because their English was not good enough.

Adapting to American culture was also a major issue for new immigrants. Even though South Korea had modernized greatly, its customs and culture were still based on

Churches like this one in New Jersey help Korean Americans adjust to life in the United States. They offer religious services in Korean and also provide a place to socialize.

Confucianism and traditional values. These put the good of the group before the good of any one member. In the United States, immigrants from Korea found a society that values individual freedom. For many Korean Americans, this made no sense.

Korean-American teens came face to face with American individualism every day in public schools. As they came to understand it, a result could be family conflict. They saw other teens hanging out with friends after school, playing sports, or working to earn money for themselves. Those activities benefited these teenagers as individuals. Korean teens might be expected to go home after school, work in a family business without pay, and then study. That was good for the entire family—but was not necessarily what the Korean-American teens came to want. The freedom that other teens had was attractive to many of the Korean Americans, but it was hard for their families to understand.

Teens Talk

In 2000, researchers from Eastern University in Pennsylvania did a study of Korean-American teenagers. Nearly all of the teens had been born in the United States, but their parents all were immigrants. The researchers noted that the parents raised their children "with the traditions of their old country. The most significant traditional Korean values . . . included respect for elders, sacrifice for the sake of the family, and the importance of education." The researchers found that the young people appreciated the sacrifices their

Sung Joo Hong and his father outside their home in Jejudo, South Korea, in 1973. A few years later, the family left for America.

One Family's Story: In Jejudo

Jejudo is the largest island in Korea. It lies about 80 miles (130 kilometers) south of the mainland. It has warm weather and beautiful scenery, including some of the highest mountains in Korea. Jejudo is often called "the Hawaii of Korea." It is a favorite destination for honeymoon couples and tourists. In the 1970s, a boy named Hong Sung Joo was living there. His parents had relatives living in the United States, and they invited the Hongs to join them there. Sung Joo's parents were people with a sense of adventure. The idea of moving to a new place was exciting. They also felt that Sung Joo and his sister would have better educational opportunities in the United States.

It's not easy for anyone to leave home and move to a foreign country. It was a difficult decision. But in the end, the Hong family decided to go.

parents had made for them. But even so, there were problems. One teen told them:

> "I feel a lot of things I go through they can't relate to. . . . I mean, they've been living here a long time, but . . . they're very clueless. . . . A lot of the problems I have I really can't tell my parents because I know they won't understand."

The study cited one typical issue between parents and their teenage children. Korean parents expect their children to obey them. Many American parents are more accepting of the fact that their teenage children may question their rules and rebel against them. Korean-American teens said their parents would not understand this.

Parents weren't the only source of problems, however. There was **racism** and discrimination as well. The teens tended to self-**segregate** at school. They would socialize mostly with each other. One teen explained, "If Korean kids hang out with white people, they call them 'bananas,' because they're yellow on the outside but white inside." When researchers asked the teens about dating, they found that the Korean Americans tended to date each other, rather than students from other backgrounds. One of them said, "There's just certain things that we don't mix. . . . We have differences. We grew up in different ways, and we have different parents, and standards are different." Another teen explained, "One thing that used to bother me was when I'd have friends over. . . . I'd take off my shoes [a Korean custom], and they wouldn't cause they're not really used to it. But Koreans . . . know each other."

Churches and Community Organizations

Unlike the earliest immigrants, the new Korean Americans had organizations they could turn to for help. Perhaps the most important were churches. As a magazine writer once put it, "The glue that holds the Korean community together in the United States is its churches." The number of Korean churches in the United States has grown rapidly. An official with the Korean World Mission Council noted that in 1965 there were two Korean churches in Chicago and only about thirty in the entire United States. By 1990, there were 140 Korean churches in Chicago and almost 2,000 in the United States.

About 65 percent of Korean Americans attend Protestant churches. Another 10 percent go to Catholic churches. Nearly all of the services are in Korean. Beyond worship, the churches provide a place to meet friends, exchange information on jobs and business, and talk to people with similar backgrounds. Korean churches are often cultural centers, too, teaching classes in Korean language, history, dance, and music.

Korean community organizations also have sprung up in larger cities across the United States. Some of these help immigrants find jobs or housing. Others help bring families from Korea to join them.

The Korean American Small Business Service Center of New York, Inc., is an organization that helps business owners with customer relations, taxes, and hiring issues. Similar groups assist Korean business owners in Chicago, Los Angeles, and Seattle.

New York City has several Asian neighborhoods. This one, in Queens, has businesses run by Korean, Japanese, and Chinese Americans.

CHAPTER FOUR

MAKING A NEW LIFE

Ki Kang was trained as an engineer in South Korea. When he came to the United States in 1969, he found a job with an engineering firm. After a while, however, he realized that his poor English kept him from advancing. While he was struggling with his job, his wife opened a small **produce** store. She was doing fairly well. Eventually, he gave up his engineering job and joined his wife's business. Together, they expanded the business and were able to open a second store.

Business Boom

The story of this couple and their success is not an unusual one. In Korean-American communities, many

Baduk is played by many Korean Americans. The game is popular with both children and adults.

Baduk

Baduk is the Korean name for a very old Asian board game. In Japan the game is called *go*. There are many variations of the game, but it is a contest of strategy and capture. *Baduk* is played on a grid, with nineteen vertical lines and nineteen horizontal lines. Players put small stones—black for one player, white for the other—at the intersections of these lines. Once a stone is placed, it can't be moved. The idea is to surround your opponent's stones, one-by-one or in groups, thereby capturing them. The game is extremely popular in Japan and Korea—and with many Korean Americans.

immigrants have made new lives by starting their own small businesses. Grocery stores, dry cleaners, fruit and vegetable stands, liquor stores, and nail salons owned by Korean Americans have sprung up across the United States. According to figures from a 2006 U.S. Census Bureau survey, more than 12 percent of Korean Americans work in their own businesses. (Overall, fewer than 7 percent of all Americans do.) Korean Americans own more than 135,000 businesses across the United States, with yearly sales of $46 billion.

Changing Names

In Korean culture, the family's name is most important, so it is always used first. The Park family in South Korea has a daughter named Se Ri (pronounced *say ree*). She has become a top professional golfer in the United States. In Korea, she is known as Park Se Ri. In the United States, she's called Se Ri Park. Many Korean Americans have made the same change, using their family name last.

A few more facts:

- 20 percent of all dry cleaning businesses in the United States are run by Korean Americans. In Chicago, the figure is 70 percent.
- Korean Americans run 45 percent of all one-hour photo shops.
- In Southern California, they own 45 percent of all liquor stores.
- In New York City, an estimated 70 percent of the Korean-American population in the labor force works in small family-owned businesses.
- New York City has 1,500 vegetable markets, 1,500 dry cleaners, 2,500 delicatessens, and 600 fish markets owned by Korean Americans.

Kimchi

Americans eat a lot of potatoes—hash browns for breakfast, French fries for lunch, and mashed potatoes for dinner. When Korean Americans sit down to eat, one dish is nearly always on the table. It's called kimchi (sometimes written kim chee). Like potatoes, it's usually served as a side dish. And like potatoes, there are lots of different ways to make it. But the most popular kind, by far, is made from cabbage, with salt and chili peppers. This spicy-hot dish may be served with any meal. Some Korean restaurants serve nothing but different kinds of spicy kimchi. In Korean-American neighborhoods, kimchi is sold on the streets from wagons or stands, like hot dogs. It's beginning to catch on as a "hot" new dish with non-Koreans, too.

Starting a business takes money. Immigrants often cannot get loans from banks because they have no **credit** history in the United States. Usually, families work at whatever jobs they can find, sometimes for several years, until they save enough to start a business of their own.

Some Koreans get start-up money through a traditional method called *kye*. It's like a club for money. A dozen or more people will form a *kye*. They will get together once a month, often for dinner at a member's home. Every member puts a sum of money (perhaps $50 to $150) into a fund. And once a month, one member of the *kye* gets the money in the fund. The only rule is that everyone must keep contributing until everyone has taken the money home once.

Neighborhood Problems

Korean Americans often started their businesses in poor or run-down areas. There were two reasons for this. First, the cost to rent or purchase property in these areas was low. Second, many businesses had left these areas, so there was less **competition**. The population of these poor neighborhoods was often heavily African American. The successes of Korean businesses in black neighborhoods—and some cultural differences—have led to anger, resentment, and sometimes violence.

Signs of Trouble

Olney is a neighborhood in northern Philadelphia. Many Korean-American businesses are located there. Newly arrived and elderly Koreans coming to shop in Olney often got confused or lost. In 1986, a community group raised money and asked the city to add Korean translations to the street signs in the neighborhood. The government agreed, and the signs went up. But no one asked the other citizens of Olney for their opinion. People who had lived there for a long time became angry. They spray-painted the Korean signs and later voted to have them removed. The language and cultural barriers between the two groups was—and still is—a big problem.

Unemployment is high in poor neighborhoods. When a new business opens, people living there hope to get jobs. But Korean business owners rarely hire them. Their stores are almost always family businesses. Parents, children, and other relatives run them and work there. If someone outside the family is hired, it is often another Korean American.

The business owners rarely live in the neighborhood where their store is located. (Newly arrived Korean Americans very often live in communities with other Korean Americans. When they can, some move to areas which they believe offer better schools for their children.) This, too, often causes resentment among the people who live, shop, and send their children to school in the neighborhood where the store is.

Korean customs and culture cause problems in these inner-city neighborhoods as well. Americans are used to getting a smile and a "Hey, how are you today?" when they

One Family's Story: In Anchorage

In November 1981, having left Jejudo, Sung Joo arrived in Anchorage, Alaska, with his parents and younger sister. The family found an apartment in a housing project near an Air Force base. Sung Joo remembers that the apartment would shake when the jets flew overhead. Jejudo's climate was fairly mild, and they were not prepared for the extreme cold and nearly constant darkness of the Alaskan winter. They soon had to buy what Sung Joo called "moon boots and jumpsuits."

Sung Joo entered school as a fifth grader, knowing little English. A special teacher worked with Sung Joo and some other students a few hours a week. The rest of the time he was in regular classes.

"I sat in the back of the class and wondered why I was there," he remembers. "I'd watch the teacher's face to see if she was talking to me. I spent a lot of time looking out the window, daydreaming, waiting for the bell to ring." He watched the other kids in order to learn what to do and when.

"Everything was so different from Korea," he says. "Kickball and football were brand new to me." There was a lot of miscommunication, and sometimes conflict would result. "Mostly," Sung Joo remembers, "they didn't know what to expect from me, and I didn't know what to expect from them."

As Sung Joo's English skills grew, he sometimes served as the family interpreter. He translated for them at the motor vehicle bureau, the telephone company, and the bank. After seven years, his father started his own business, cleaning carpets. Sung Joo helped with the work, with business calls at home, and with making appointments. Working in a family business, he says, "was a very common experience for kids in the Korean community."

Sung Joo graduated from high school in 1989. He had already experienced a lifetime of changes, but more were to come.

Sung Joo *(right)* with his sister in Alaska in the 1980s.

Source: U.S. Bureau of the Census, 2006 estimates

go into a neighborhood store. Koreans, however, are taught to be serious in business situations. They don't smile, and they may acknowledge a customer only with a slight nod. There are even greater problems with women. In Korean culture, it is improper for women to look men in the eye or touch them. For male customers, that means a female shop clerk won't look at them and will put their change on the counter instead of handing it to them.

For Korean Americans, these are good manners and signs of proper upbringing. But to African Americans, a Korean-American shopkeeper's behavior may seem rude, disrespectful, and insulting. To them, it seems that the Korean Americans are taking money from the neighborhood, but do not live there and contribute nothing to it.

These feelings came to a head in New York City in 1990. African Americans organized a four-month-long boycott of Korean-American businesses in a part of Brooklyn. They

In April 1992, three days of rioting destroyed more than 2,300 Korean-owned businesses in Los Angeles. Businesses in this shopping mall were among them.

passed out leaflets urging blacks not to do business "with people who do not look like us, do not live in our community, and do not care about us." During the boycott, several people were attacked, some windows were broken, and several arrests were made.

But things were much worse in Los Angeles two years later. A Korean-American woman, Soon Ja Du, who owned an inner-city grocery store shot and killed a fifteen-year-old black girl. Du claimed the girl had stolen a carton of orange juice. Du went to trial and was found guilty, but she was not sent to jail. At the same time, four white police officers who had been accused of savagely beating a black man named Rodney King were tried and found not guilty. The black community erupted in violence. Rioting lasted for three days. Fifty-four people died and more than two thousand were injured. Nearly 4,500 businesses were damaged or destroyed, and 2,300 of them were owned by Korean Americans. Many of them did not re-open.

Making a new life became much harder for the Korean Americans whose stores and businesses were destroyed. Life was also harder for the residents of that Los Angeles neighborhood. The goods and services supplied by the Korean Americans were gone. The future for both groups would have both high points and low.

While a number of Korean Americans in New York, Los Angeles, and other cities had problems, many of them were successful as well. And their children—many of whom were born in the United States—would tend to be even more successful.

Cooking food right at the table is just part of the service in this Korean restaurant.

CHAPTER FIVE

CHANGING THE AMERICAN CULTURE

John Adams, the second president of the United States, once wrote, "I must study politics and war that my sons may . . . study mathematics and **philosophy** . . . in order to give their children a right to study painting, poetry, music, [and] **architecture**." Adams wrote that more than two hundred years ago. But his words could easily describe the generations of new immigrants from Korea.

Those who immigrated after U.S. immigration law changed in 1965 were the first large group of new Korean Americans. Many of these people had experienced war or its **aftermath**. In the United States, they worked hard and saved their money. A great many started their own businesses. Families often worked up to fourteen hours a day.

Their children are the next generation of today's Korean Americans. Some of them were born in Korea, and others were born in the United States. They grew up speaking Korean at home but English in school. Many worked in family businesses as young people. Some stayed in those businesses as adults. Others went on to college—studying mathematics, philosophy, and more—and they found careers in other professions.

Their children are still another generation of new Korean Americans. Few of them have ever been to Korea, and they know it only through stories. English is the main language in their homes, and some of them struggle to speak Korean. They may marry other Korean Americans but are just as likely to marry someone from another background. And they are working in many fields, including government, science, sports, and (as Adams wrote) painting, poetry, music, and architecture.

Each of these generations has changed the American culture. Just as surely, however, those generations have been changed by America.

Changing America

In New York City in the 1990s, the Korean population grew to over 100,000. Restaurants serving Korean dishes, markets catering to Korean tastes, and businesses run by Korean families filled several blocks near Broadway in the center of Manhattan. Similar large Korean-American communities developed in other parts of the city, including the Flushing neighborhood in the borough of Queens.

Contributing to America: Jhoon Rhee

He can do one hundred push-ups in less than a minute. He also created National Teacher Appreciation Day. It was signed into law by President Ronald Reagan in 1986. His name is Jhoon Goo Rhee. He is one of the world's greatest masters of tae kwon do. Born in Korea in 1932, Rhee came to the United States in 1956. He studied engineering at the University of Texas and began teaching martial arts. He now has more than sixty tae kwon do studios across the country. Rhee is given much of the credit for making martial arts popular in the United States. He worked with movie star Bruce Lee and former boxing champion Muhammad Ali. When teaching his younger students, Rhee demands excellence in the classroom as well as the gym. He requires his students to keep a B average or better. He was an adviser to the President's Council on Physical Fitness and Sports from 1988 to 1991. In 2000, the U.S. Immigration and Naturalization Service and the National Immigration Forum compiled a list of the 203 most important American immigrants. The list included Albert Einstein, Alexander Graham Bell, and Jhoon Rhee.

Jhoon Rhee demonstrates his tae kwon do skills while balancing a glass on his head.

An area of Chicago was once called "Andersonville" because many immigrants from **Scandinavia** lived there and Anderson is a common Scandinavian last name. Today it's called "Korean Town." Young-Woon Lee, the pastor of a Korean church in the area, says, "You can live here and never need to speak English."

Without question, however, the "capital" of Korean America is Los Angeles. An article in *Newsweek* magazine in 1975 noted that a new community had grown up along Olympic Boulevard. "It's called Koreatown," the magazine said. "What used to be Mexican-American, Japanese, and Jewish stores are now mostly Korean, with giant oriental letters spread across their low-slung storefronts." Koreatown continued to grow after 1975. Today it has the largest concentration of Korean Americans in the United States, with a population estimated as high as 130,000 people.

Working, Studying, Stereotyping

Working hard, sacrificing for children, and valuing education are all characteristics of Korean Americans. And it is true that many of these immigrants have become successful, and their children have usually done very well in school.

This has led to **stereotyping**. Some people believe that all Korean Americans own thriving businesses and send their children to Harvard. But, of course, they don't. According to the Census Bureau's 2006 American Community Survey, more than 78,000 Korean Americans work in construction, fishing, maintenance, and similar occupations. Many Korean Americans resent the very high expectations that come with the positive stereotyping of Korean immigrants and their descendants (the tendency to view Korean Americans as what is sometimes termed a "model minority").

Being Changed by America

The early generations of Korean-American families often included extended family members. Grandparents, parents, and older children frequently shared a single household. This follows Korean custom: the eldest son in the family stays with his parents and cares for them as they grow older. The 1980 U.S. Census

Contributing to America: Linda Sue Park

Her first published work was a short poem that appeared in *Trailblazer* magazine. She was paid only a dollar for it, but she was, after all, only nine years old. Linda Sue Park has been paid a lot more for her writing since then.

Park's parents immigrated to the United States in the 1950s. They decided to leave their old ways behind. Park says, "My parents thought the best way to help us succeed was to become very American, which meant only speaking English at home."

Years later, when she had children of her own, Park wanted them to know about their Korean **heritage**. Park had to learn about it herself. While reading and talking to her parents, she decided to write a book.

Since then she has written several novels for young people. Each one is set in Korea, at a different time in history. Her third book, *A Single Shard*, won the 2002 Newbery Medal. This prize is given each year by the American Library Association for the most distinguished children's book. Park was the first Korean American to win the award.

found that the average Korean-American household had 4.3 people. The national average then was 2.7 people.

By 2006, this had changed. The Census Bureau's American Community Survey found that the average size of families across the country was 3.20 people. That was nearly identical to the average size of a Korean-American family: 3.28 people. Korean-American children were growing up and leaving home—not staying with their parents.

One Family's Story: In San Diego

Sung Joo started college in Alaska in 1990. Soon after that, his father moved the family to Northridge, California, near Los Angeles. Sung Joo remained in Alaska to complete his degree. He graduated from the University of Alaska in 1994. He moved to San Diego, California. There he enrolled in a master's degree program at Pacific College to study **acupuncture**. This is a traditional form of medicine that has been used in Asia for more than two thousand years.

In San Diego, Sung Joo met and fell in love with an American classmate named Rachel. When he introduced Rachel to his parents, his mother said, "Love is love, and in love, there are no boundaries between countries." And his father added, "She is beautiful. You are a lucky man."

Rachel also studied acupuncture. They married after Sung Joo graduated. Sung Joo's sister and mother taught Rachel to make Sung Joo's favorite Korean foods. Then, Sung Joo says, "In 1998, God blessed us, and our daughter So Ra was born. I had started my own family in America!"

Sung Joo (in the blue vest) with Rachel, his parents, and his younger brother in San Diego.

Contributing to America: Sarah Chang

Sarah Chang's parents were both musicians in South Korea. They moved to Philadelphia in 1979 to continue their studies. Sarah was born in 1980. Her father remembers that as a very young child Sarah could play one-finger tunes on the piano. She wanted to play the violin too, he said, but "I wouldn't let her put her sticky fingers on my violin."

When she was four, Sarah's parents gave her a tiny violin of her own. Her father said, "She seemed naturally able to play." She was accepted into classes at Temple University's Center for Gifted Children at the age of six. An instructor said Chang was "the most phenomenal talent I have seen in my years of teaching." When she was eight, Chang performed at the Philadelphia Academy of Music. In 1990, at age ten, she played with the New York Philharmonic Orchestra.

Since then, Sarah Chang has played with orchestras around the world. She is recognized as one of classical music's most exciting performers.

Sarah Chang practices for a concert in Tel Aviv, Israel, in 2005. She is among the world's top violinists.

Dating and marriage customs have been changed by American life, too. In recent surveys, Korean-American women in college said they often preferred dating non-Korean men. Marrying outside the Korean-American community has become increasingly common as well. Housing, language, dating, and marriage are just some of the ways that America has changed Korean immigrants.

Colorful dancers perform during the Opening Ceremonies of the 1988 Summer Olympic Games in Seoul, South Korea. The event gave many Korean Americans an increased sense of pride in their Korean heritage.

CHAPTER SIX

LOOKING TO THE FUTURE

By the 2000s, immigration from South Korea to the United States had dropped sharply. A major reason for this decline was a change that had taken place in South Korea itself and that had actually started during the 1980s. By the end of the twentieth and the beginning of the twenty-first century, the country's economy was no longer struggling. In fact, South Korea had become an economic power in Asia—and the rest of the world as well. Because of its economic growth, it became known as "an Asian tiger." It also modernized its education system. South Korea was the first country in the world to provide high-speed Internet access to every elementary, middle, and high school. In essence, emigration from South Korea slowed because there were fewer reasons for people to leave their native country.

Reverse Migration

For some Korean Americans, the 1988 Olympics were more than just a source of pride. When they watched the Games, Koreans living outside Korea saw a modern, progressive country. It was much different from the one they may have left in the 1960s or 1970s. The Olympics started a small reverse **migration** movement. Koreans who had immigrated to the United States began going back to Korea. By the mid-1990s, about five thousand people were returning each year.

In the United States, the Korean-American community began to look back at where it had come from and to look ahead to where it might go. A number of events helped these new Americans take greater pride in their heritage.

The 1988 Summer Olympics were held in South Korea. This was a source of great pride for many Korean Americans. Their homeland became the center of worldwide attention. Julie Hong was 21 at the time and living in Los Angeles. She left Korea when she was four years old. She said, "It's great to see on television how beautiful it is, and what it's like in Korea."

Japan and South Korea co-hosted the World Cup in 2002. This international soccer tournament is often called the most-watched sporting event on earth. It was another source of pride for Koreans—and for Korean Americans.

In 2006, Ban Ki-Moon, a South Korean diplomat, was named Secretary General of the United Nations. For many Korean Americans, this achievement by a Korean leader was a source of pride in their heritage. Lim Myungsook is an administrator at a high school in California. She clipped news articles about Ban and put them up on the school's bulletin boards. "He's a good role model," she said. "If you work hard and study well . . . you will make progress."

The Act of One Person

In April 2007, horrible news came from the campus of a university in Virginia. A gunman killed thirty-three students and instructors at Virginia Tech. Fifteen others were wounded. The gunman then killed himself. He was a Korean-born former student named Seung-Hui Cho.

As the news was breaking, a *Washington Post* reporter talked to Yung Yang, a Korean American who lived near Washington, D.C. She cried as she told the reporter, "I am so sorry about this. Every Korean person is so very sorry." Many Korean-American churches held prayer services. Messages of sorrow were sent to Virginia Tech.

One California reporter objected to this. Rene Astudillo heads the Asian American Journalists Association. She did not want Korean Americans to accept any blame for the tragedy. Astudillo said, "This is the act of one person . . . from South Korea. There is no reason for us to say we're sorry for that."

But Korean Americans did worry that they would be blamed. The *Los Angeles Times* interviewed an African-American community leader named Earl Hutchinson. "They [Korean Americans] know there's a rush to judgment about foreigners," he said. "Is that fair? No. But the reality is there's a long history of stereotyping Asians in this country."

Maintain and Reach Out

Korean Americans want to be proud of their homeland and maintain their language and cultural heritage. At the same time, they want to be seen as individuals, not stereotyped

In a candlelight ceremony,
Virginia Tech students remembered those
killed and wounded by a Korean-born gunman in 2007.

members of a group. Korean Americans want to reach out, participate, and become completely integrated into American life.

Language has often stopped Korean immigrants from interacting with other Americans. In addition, many of them worked long, hard hours and had little time or energy for other activities. Cultural differences could play a role as well. The director of a Korean-American social services agency in New York City pointed out that American culture values participation: people are often involved in their local schools, attend and speak out at local government meetings, and in general openly express their opinions. But in Korean culture, that kind of participation has traditionally not been valued in the same way.

Rebuilding Koreatown

The 1992 riots destroyed thousands of Korean-American businesses in Los Angeles. In the early 2000s, however, Koreatown began to bounce back. Today, it is a tourist destination. New stores, apartments, and nightclubs are attracting young people. Traditional noodle shops are now side-by-side with Internet cafes, Korean karaoke clubs called *noraebangs*, and Korean barbeque stands.

Traditional Korean values were tested by the boycott of Korean-American businesses in New York in 1990. They were changed by the Los Angeles riots in 1992. Korean Americans were forced to look more closely at themselves and their relations with other Americans—particularly African Americans. Nancy Ablemann and John Lie wrote a book called *Blue Dreams: Korean Americans and the Los Angeles Riots*. They described the change this way:

"There was a definable surge in Korean-American political participation after the riots. Several young

Korean Americans we met were so deeply affected that they quit or abandoned plans for more **lucrative** jobs to enter community service—as members of Korean-American organizations, volunteers in advocacy groups, or staff members of community organizations."

Improving Business and Race Relations

Yang-Il Kim was one of those who reached out and tried to make things better. He took steps to improve relations between Korean-American store owners and their communities. As chairman of the National Korean-American Grocers Association in Los Angeles, he urged Koreans to hire local people whenever possible. Kim suggested other simple changes, such as saying "Hi!" when customers walk in, and speaking English as much as possible.

Other organizations are working to improve race relations. The Korean Produce Association in New York is one example. It was started because grocers felt they were being mistreated by the suppliers of their fruits and vegetables. The association helped its members settle those problems with suppliers. But it also worked with the African-American community during the 1990 boycott. Pyong Gap Min, a New York City sociologist and author, says that "in recent years, Black-Korean conflicts have largely vanished."

In 1993, the Korea Society in New York began a "Kids to Korea" program. The program selected sixteen African-American high school students from New York City and Los Angeles. They went to South Korea, where they met and visited with Korean teens. They learned about Korea's people, culture, and history. The hope was that the students would share what they learned with others in their neighborhoods back home. The program was successful and is continuing.

The Littlest Immigrants Grow Up

Thousands of Korean infants have been adopted by foreign parents since the 1950s. Some are now teenagers; others are middle-aged adults. In the United States, most of these Korean adoptees (KADs, for short) grew up in white, middle-class or upper-class families. It wasn't always easy for them, however. Some experienced racism. Many felt confused about who they were—white or Asian. They didn't know their real names, family background, or medical history. KADs felt shut off from other Korean Americans because they could not speak the language and knew nothing of the culture. Some American parents tried to bridge this gap by sending their KADs to Korean schools or camps. Other KADs visited Korea to learn more about their birth heritage. Several U.S. cities now have support groups where KADs can meet and share their experiences.

Assimilation and Preservation

The United States has often been called a "melting pot." People from many countries and many cultures come to the United States and get blended together. This is called **assimilation**. Over time, immigrants become a little less like "them" and a little more like "us."

Many Korean Americans worry about this. Some first generation immigrants, who never learned much English, find they can't talk to their Americanized grandchildren who know little Korean. The newest generations, born in the United States, have few direct connections to Korea. These new immigrants are finding ways to preserve their cultural identity.

An obvious sign of this is the growth of Korean language schools. In 1990, one survey found there were 490 Korean language schools in the United States. And the growth is

One Family's Story: In Rochester and Seattle

In 1999, Sung Joo moved to Rochester, New York, to be near Rachel's family. There they started their own acupuncture practice. Their daughter, So Ra, got to know her American grandparents. She grew up speaking both English and Korean. Her grandfather had a tank of tropical fish. When she was three, So Ra always talked about the *gogi*. *Gogi* is Korean for fish.

In 2003, Rachel's parents moved to Seattle. A year later, Sung Joo and his family followed. Sung Joo says, "Many Korean Americans live in Seattle, and our daughter has opportunities to learn about Korean language and culture. On weekends she goes to a Korean language school. She also takes tae kwon do classes and plays [the traditional Asian board game] *baduk*. As a father, I try to pass on my Korean traditions as much as I can."

Sung Joo hopes to take his whole family to Korea one day. He wants them to see Jejudo and to meet his grandmother and other relatives. He wants them to see the places they know only from the stories he has told them.

Looking at his overall experience as an immigrant, Sung Joo says, "I still face some discrimination. I look different, eat different food, and have an accent. Sometimes I think everyone in the world should live in a different country for two years or more. This would make the world a more understanding place."

As a Korean American today, Sung Joo says: "I admire my father, who was brave to forge a new life so far away from Korea. I respect my mother, who held the family together during hard times. We have become part of America and its culture."

Sung Joo *(fourth from right, standing)* and Rachel *(next to him)* in Seattle, with the Korean and American sides of their family.

not limited to elementary and high school students. Several American universities—including Brigham Young, Columbia, Cornell, Harvard, the University of Hawaii, and the University of Washington—offer degree programs in Korean language and Korean studies.

Part of the Community

Slowly, Korean Americans are becoming less isolated. They are moving from being a separate group to being an active part of the communities where they live. Instead of keeping their heritage to themselves, they are reaching out and sharing it.

One example is the Korean cultural festival held in Seattle each fall. It is called Ch'uSok, the Harvest Moon Festival. Ch'uSok is a traditional Korean holiday of thanksgiving. During the three-day celebration, many Koreans take off from work and get together with family and friends. They enjoy lavish meals filled with traditional foods. (More Koreans travel for Ch'uSok get-togethers than at any other time of year.) The Seattle Ch'uSok festival includes tae kwon do demonstrations, movies, and student art exhibits. Korean music, dancing, and, of course, food are all part of the celebration. The festival has become more than a gathering for Korean Americans. It has become a tourist attraction, drawing crowds of people of all races. Ch'uSok provides social and economic benefits to both Korean Americans and the greater Seattle area. Moving into the future while honoring the past is the goal for many Korean Americans today.

FACTS ABOUT KOREAN AMERICANS

Characteristic	Korean Americans	Percentage for Korean Americans	Total U.S. Population	Percentage for U.S. Population
Total population	1,335,075		299,398,485	
Male	614,135	46%	146,705,258	49%
Female	720,940	54%	152,693,227	51%
Median age (years)	35		36	
Under 5 years old	66,754	5%	20,957,894	7%
18 years and over	1,054,709	79%	224,548,864	75%
65 years and over	106,806	8%	35,927,818	12%
Average family size	3		3	
Number of households	446,530		111,617,402	
Owner-occupied housing units	218,800	49%	74,783,659	67%
Renter-occupied housing units	227,730	51%	36,833,743	33%
People age 25 and over with high school diploma or higher	811,308	91%	164,729,046	84%
People age 25 and over with bachelor's degree or higher	472,520	53%	52,948,622	27%
Foreign born	1,002,100	75%	37,547,789	13%
Number of people who speak a language other than English at home (population 5 years and older)	1,012,150	80%	55,807,878	20%
Median family income	$61,592		$58,526	
Per capita income	$25,639		$25,267	
Individuals living below the poverty level	186,911	14%	38,921,803	13%

Source: U.S. Bureau of the Census, 2006 American Community Survey estimates

GLOSSARY

acupuncture: An ancient method of relieving pain and treating illnesses by inserting needles into specific places in the body.

aftermath: Things that happen as the result of an event.

architecture: The art, science, and profession of designing buildings.

assimilation: The process by which people who have moved to another country adopt the customs and behaviors of the people in their new environment.

boycotting: Refusing to buy goods or services from a person, company, or nation.

census: An official count of the people living in an area; the U.S. Constitution requires a census count of the number of people in the United States every ten years.

civil rights: The basic rights that a government must guarantee for its citizens.

civilian: A person who is not in the military.

Communist: Referring to a political and economic system (Communism) in which a powerful government owns land, factories, and other businesses and centrally plans a country's economy. People work for government-owned and government-run enterprises. The word Communist also refers to a person who is a follower of Communism.

competition: The act of trying to win, or gain an advantage over, or move ahead of someone else; a contest.

credit: Trusting someone to repay borrowed money.

culture: The beliefs, customs, and way of life of a group of people.

discrimination: Treating people unfairly because of race, age, or other reasons.

dynasty: A series of rulers from the same family.

economy: The way a country makes and uses its money, natural resources, goods, and services.

emigration: The act of leaving one's own country, usually to settle elsewhere.

engineer: A person who plans and builds roads, bridges, buildings, and other structures, or plans and builds machinery and equipment (for example, computers or airplanes).

harassed: Bullied, teased, or discriminated against.

heritage: Ideas, customs, manners, and language handed down from one generation to the next.

hermit: Someone who intentionally lives apart from other people.

hypothetical: Made up but intended to be typical of a real-life situation.

immigrant: A person who travels to another country, usually to settle there.

immigration: The act of traveling to and entering a new country, usually to settle there.

interpreter: A person who translates one language into another language.

lucrative: Something that produces a great deal of money.

manufacturing: Making things using machinery.

matchmaker: A person who arranges for people to meet so that they may marry.

migration: The act of moving from one place to another.

militant: Aggressive; engaging in armed actions.

missionaries: People who teach and spread their religion, usually in foreign countries.

oppressive: Harsh; allowing very little liberty.

peninsula: A piece of land that is surrounded by water on three sides.

philosopher: A person who develops a philosophy, or way of thinking about the world, or who studies philosophy.

philosophy: A system of beliefs about the basic nature of life, knowledge, matter, and reality; the study of these systems of beliefs.

plantation: A very large farm.

preference: Something that is liked best; first choice.

produce: (noun) Farm products, usually fruits and vegetables.

protested: Objected to or complained about.

quota: Maximum number or amount; immigration quotas refer to fixed maximum numbers of people who are permitted to enter a country each year.

racism: Discrimination based on a person's or a group's race.

refugee: Someone who seeks or takes shelter in a foreign country, especially to avoid war, political persecution, or religious persecution in his or her native country.

resentment: Having feelings of anger, bitterness, or unhappiness.

retail: Selling products directly to customers in small amounts.

Scandinavia: A group of countries in northern Europe that includes Norway, Sweden, and Denmark.

segregate: To separate, often according to race or color.

shambles: A state of destruction.

stereotyping: Making oversimplified, and often unfavorable, characterizations of a person or group of people.

turbulent: Marked by unrest, disturbances, or violence.

unions: Organizations made up of groups of workers who act together to get such benefits as higher pay or better working conditions.

TO FIND OUT MORE

Further Reading

Choi, Anne Soon. *Korean Americans*. New York: Facts on File, 2007.

Ingram, Scott. *Korean Americans*. Milwaukee, WI: World Almanac Library, 2006.

Martin, Jennifer C. *The Korean Americans*. San Diego, CA: Lucent Books, 2005.

Na, An. *A Step from Heaven*. New York: Penguin Young Readers Group, 2002. (A novel about a Korean girl and her family trying to learn English and adjust to American life.)

Noonan, Sheila Smith. *Korean Immigration*. Philadelphia: Mason Crest, 2003.

Peterson, Tiffany. *Korean Americans*. Chicago: Heinemann Library, 2003.

Websites

www.calstatela.edu/centers/ckaks
The Center for Korean American and Korean Studies (CKAKS) is part of California State University. This site has Census data, news about the Korean-American community, and links to related sites

www.clickkorea.org
This site includes news and current events, information on books about Korea, Korean language lessons, and more. The arts section has pictures of Korean painting, crafts, and sculpture.

www.cynthialeitichsmith.com/lit_resources/diversity/asian_am/Korean.html
Cynthia Leitich Smith is an author who also reviews books for young adults. This site contains a list of books about Korea and Korean Americans.

www.falcon.jmu.edu/~ramseyil/mulkoreanamer.htm
This site features a list of books for young people about Korea and Korean Americans. The list includes novels, poetry, and history and was compiled by educators at James Madison University.

www.geocities.com/mokkim/kafacts.html
This site includes facts and statistics about Korean Americans.

BIBLIOGRAPHY

The author found these sources especially helpful when researching this volume:

Foster, Jenny Ryun, Stewart, Frank, and Fenkl, Heinz Insu, editors. *Century of the Tiger: One Hundred Years of Korean Culture in America, 1903-2003*. Honolulu: University of Hawaii Press, 2003.

Kim, Ilpyong, editor. *Korean-Americans: Past, Present, and Future.* Elizabeth, NJ: Hollym International Publishing, 2004.

Min, Pyong Gap. *Ethnic Solidarity for Economic Survival: Korean Greengrocers in New York City*. New York: Russell Sage Foundation, 2008.

Park, Kyeyoung. *Korean American Dream: Immigrants and Small Business in New York City*. Ithaca, NY: Cornell University Press, 1997.

Patterson, Wayne. *The Korean Frontier in America: Immigration to Hawaii, 1896-1910*. Honolulu: University of Hawaii Press, 1994.

Swan, Charlie, and Weissbrot, Jill. "A Generation in Transition: A Study of Korean-American Youth." Eastern University Publications: *Electronic Magazine of Multicultural Education*, Spring 2000.

Yuh, Ji-Yeon. *Beyond the Shadow of Camptown: Korean Military Brides in America*. New York: New York University Press, 2002.

Various articles in the *New York Times, Los Angeles Times,* and *Washington Post*.

The author conducted personal interviews with Hong Sung Joo, who is quoted in this book, and the author and the publisher wish to thank him for his cooperation.

Notes:

Chapter 6:

Page 64, "It's great to see on television...." "Los Angeles Journal: Olympics Bring Pride to Koreatown," *New York Times*, September 19, 1988.

Page 64, "He's a good role model...." "Korean Americans Proud of Ban Ki-Moon in U.N. Post," *San Francisco Chronicle*, December 12, 2006.

Page 65, "This is the act of one person...." "Ethnicity Brings Unwelcome Focus," *Los Angeles Times*, April 19, 2007.

Page 68, "In recent years, Black-Korean...." "In the Produce Aisle, Solidarity for Korean Grocers," *New York Times*, September 5, 2008.

All websites were accessible as of March 8, 2009.

INDEX

Page numbers in **boldface** are illustrations, tables, and charts.

About the Series Consultant

Judith Ann Warner is a Professor of Sociology and Criminal Justice at Texas A&M International University (TAMIU), located in Laredo, Texas, near the U.S.-Mexico border. She has specialized in the study of race and ethnic relations, focusing on new immigrants to the United States and their social incorporation into American society. Professor Warner is the editor of and contributed a number of essays to *Battleground Immigration* (2009), a collection of essays on immigration and related national security issues. Recognition of her work includes the 2007 Distance Educator of the Year Award and the 1991 Scholar of the Year Award at TAMIU.

About the Author

William David Thomas lives in Rochester, New York. Thomas has written books for children and young adults, software documentation, annual reports, magazine articles, speeches, and training programs. His four-book series *My American Government* received a social studies award nomination from the Association of Educational Publishers in 2008. This book is for Logan, Rachel, and Abigail. It is Thomas's first book for Marshall Cavendish Benchmark.